D1055505

GEOCACHE
SURPRISE

BY JAKE MADDOX

ILLUSTRATED BY SEAN TIFFANY

text by Eric Stevens

STONE ARCH BOOKS
a capstone imprint

J
MAD

Jake Maddox books are published by Stone Arch Books
A Capstone Imprint
151 Good Counsel Drive, P.O. Box 669
Mankato, Minnesota 56002
www.capstonepub.com

*Library of Congress Cataloging-in-Publication Data is available on the
Library of Congress website.*

Library Binding: 978-1-4342-2600-6

Summary: Tim is disappointed when his best friend wants to spend their
last day of summer geocaching. But a competition might make things
interesting!

Art Director: Kay Fraser
Graphic Designer: Hilary Wacholz
Production Specialist: Michelle Biedscheid

Photo Credits: ShutterStock/D_V (p. 71), Sean Tiffany (cover, p. 1)

Printed in the United States of America in Stevens Point, Wisconsin.
092010
005934WZS11

TABLE OF CONTENTS

CHAPTER 1

SUMMER'S OVER

Tim Ricardo hadn't had a great summer. For one thing, his three best friends were all at camp. He was the only one still at home in Pebble Junction. Plus, he was saving up to buy a computer, so he'd worked almost every weekday at his dad's hardware store.

On weekends, Tim always planned to go to the beach. But it always seemed like whenever he got there, it was cloudy and raining.

"Rainiest summer ever," his dad said the last Sunday morning of the summer. "We broke the record set back in 1952."

"Great," Tim said. "That's one record I hope we never break again."

"There is good news," Dad said. "Tomorrow is Labor Day, and the paper says clear skies all day and night. The weather will be perfect for the fireworks and barbecue down at the beach."

"Finally," Tim said. "It's the last day of the summer, and I get to spend it at the beach."

"And isn't Brent Saber back in town now?" Dad said.

Brent Saber was Tim's best friend, but he'd been gone all summer at Camp Bluesky, a computer camp way up north.

"Hey, that's right," Tim said. "The bus from camp must have dropped him off this morning."

"I'm sure the Sabers will be at the fireworks," Dad said. He grabbed the newspaper and headed for the couch. "Should be a great last day of the summer."

CHAPTER 2

JUST IN TIME

The Labor Day fireworks in Pebble Junction were an annual celebration that had been going on for almost a hundred years. The fireworks were held down at the beach, right on the harbor. Before the fireworks, there was a big barbecue.

Everyone in town went. It was something Tim looked forward to every year. It was the perfect way to celebrate the last day of summer.

The big barbecue started at noon on Labor Day. Tim's family got there at about 11:30 and grabbed a great spot to picnic. They set up their chairs and blankets halfway between the food stand and the gentle waves from the lake.

"I knew we should have gotten here earlier," Dad said. He put his hands on his hips and looked at the long line at the food stand. "They better not run out of spicy sausage."

Mom patted his shoulder. "Don't worry, dear," she said. She winked at Tim.

"I guess I'll go look for Brent," Tim said. "The water looks great, so I hope he brought his body-surf board."

"I'll grab a couple of hot dogs for you," Dad said. "Come back in a few minutes."

Mom waved as Tim started off across the sand.

The beach was packed. Tim had to walk slowly and weave around blanket after blanket. Before he'd gone a hundred yards, he'd seen at least ten families he knew.

Finally, Tim spotted Brent's dad. At over six and a half feet tall, he wasn't hard to find. He was standing on a blanket near the forest.

"Hey, Mr. Saber," Tim called out. He started walking over. Brent's dad spotted him and smiled.

"You're just in time," Brent's dad said when Tim reached him. No one else was there.

"Where's Brent?" Tim asked. "He's back from computer camp, right?"

"Like I was saying," Mr. Saber said, "you're just in time. Brent will be back in a minute. He went to meet up with Paul and Tyrone."

"The twins are here too?" Tim said. "Cool. It's nice to have my best friends back in town."

"And when they get here, we'll start the competition," Mr. Saber said.

"What competition?" Tim asked.

Just then, Brent and the twins walked up. Mr. Saber ignored Tim's question.

To Tim's surprise, the other boys weren't dressed right for the beach. Instead of wearing shorts and T-shirts, they were all in jeans and hiking boots.

Mr. Saber said, "Look who showed up while you were in the lunch line."

"Hey, Tim!" Brent said. He gave Tim a high five. "Did you have a good summer?"

Tim shrugged. "Terrible, actually," he said. "It rained here every single weekend. I didn't get to the beach one time."

"I heard," Brent said. He frowned. "Well, up north the weather was great."

Tim smiled. "Like you need great weather to goof around with computers all summer," he said.

"We weren't at the computers all summer," Paul said. "Like I told you, we went geocaching a lot."

Tim scratched his ear. "You went what?" he asked.

"Geocaching," Brent said. "That's what we're going to do right now, too."

"Oh, no way," Tim said. He held up his beach towel. "We're going swimming and bodysurfing. Then we're eating hot dogs and watching fireworks. It's the last day of summer."

"Trust me," Brent said. "You'll love geocaching. It's even more fun than bodysurfing."

Tim looked across the crowded beach at the waves crashing on the lakeshore. He didn't know what geocaching was, but he didn't plan to let it stop him from hitting those waves.

CHAPTER 3

TREASURE HUNT

"I'm sure geocaching is a great time," Tim said. "But I am not spending my last day of freedom before eighth grade starts hiking through the woods."

Brent laughed. "It's more than just hiking," he said. "I promise. You'll really love it!"

"I thought we were going to spend the day at the beach," Tim said. "You know, like we usually do on Labor Day."

"I know," Brent said. "But Dad got really excited about geocaching. He even bought something to give out as a prize. And we'll make it back in time for the fireworks. I swear."

Tim gave a deep sigh. "Okay," he said. "I'll do it. As long as you promise that as soon as we're done, we're back to the beach."

"You got it," Brent said, smiling.

Paul pulled something from the pocket of his jeans. It looked like a cell phone.

"I'll send the coordinates to you guys," Mr. Saber said. "Brent already has them in his device."

Tim watched as Paul, Tyrone, Brent, and Mr. Saber gathered together in a huddle. They had three of the devices.

The four talked over each other, so Tim couldn't make out any of the conversation. Finally, he'd had enough.

"Hey!" he shouted. The others stopped talking and turned to him. "What are you all talking about?" Tim asked, in a quieter voice.

The others stopped and turned to face Tim. "Haven't you been listening?" Brent said. "We're talking about geocaching?"

Tim stared back at Brent. "Right. Geocaching," he said. "I know that. But no one has explained what exactly geocaching is," he added.

"It's very simple," Paul said. He held out his device so Tim could see it. It was the size of a cell phone and had a small screen and fewer buttons than a phone.

"This is a GPS device," Paul explained. "It's connected to satellites, and it knows the coordinates where you are, no matter where you go."

"Plus," Tyrone said, "you can tell it the coordinates of a geocache. Then it will help you find it."

"That doesn't sound very simple," Tim said. "In fact, I still don't really get it."

Brent smiled. "Think of it like we're treasure hunting," he said. He held up his own GPS device. "This is like the map, with an X to mark the spot," he said.

"Except you don't get to keep the treasure," Mr. Saber explained. "You just find it and leave it where it is, for someone else to find another day. Instead of taking it, you sign the log so people know you were there."

"Treasure hunting," Tim said, "without a treasure. Sounds . . . boring."

Brent shook his head. "Look, just give it a try, okay?" he said. "It's fun. I promise."

"And since we've got a few beginners here," Mr. Saber said, "we're going to make it more exciting."

He dug around in the bag on the Sabers' blanket and pulled out a small wrapped box. "The team of two who finds their cache first and makes it back to the picnic blanket will win this prize," Mr. Saber said, holding up the box.

"I like prizes," Tim said. "What is it?"

Mr. Saber smiled. "Let's put it this way," he said. "It's something Tyrone, Paul, and Brent used a lot this summer."

It's got to be a computer, Tim thought.

"Okay," he said. "Who's on my team?"

"We better split up the twins," Brent said. "To make it fair. I'll take Tyrone, you take Paul."

"Sounds good," Tim said. "When do we start?"

"Right after we eat," Brent said. He took a bite from his foot-long hot dog.

"Oh, right," Tim said. He put a hand on his stomach. "I knew I forgot something. I'll be back after I eat."

"Hey, Tim," Brent said as Tim turned to head back to his own blanket. "You'd better find something to wear on your feet instead of those flip-flops."

Tim looked at his feet. "Why?" he said. "What's wrong with my flip-flops?"

"You can't go hiking in the woods in flip-flops," Mr. Saber said.

Tim nodded and started off. "Some day at the beach this is turning out to be," he grumbled to himself.

He made it back to his family's blanket just as his dad was walking up with a big cardboard tray of food.

"Just in time," his dad called out, smiling. "What a long line! I thought I'd never reach the front." He handed Tim a hot dog. It was slightly burnt on the outside, just the way he liked it.

"Now this is what the beach is all about," Tim said.

I just wish my friends wanted to spend the day my way, he thought.

CHAPTER 4

INTO THE WOODS

After lunch, Tim was full of hot dogs and soda, and he was moving slow. He and the other boys and Mr. Saber were standing on the edge of the wooded park, just inches from the lakefront.

"Are you guys sure you wouldn't rather spend the day at the beach?" Tim asked his friends.

Brent laughed. "Yeah, I'm sure," he said. "Trust me, you'll have fun."

"But you were at camp all summer. I thought you'd want to hang out more," Tim said.

"I do," Brent said. "We're hanging out now, aren't we? Look, this will be fun, and I bet you'll love it."

Whatever, Tim thought. *I'm not going to love it. But I'm going to make sure my team wins! I need that computer.*

"Is everyone ready?" Mr. Saber asked.

"I'm ready," Tim said.

"I'm glad you found some better shoes to wear," Mr. Saber said, looking at Tim's feet.

Tim looked down. He'd grabbed an old pair of sneakers from his dad's car before joining the others.

The sneakers weren't perfect for hiking, but they were better than flip-flops.

"I'm ready too," Brent said.

Paul and Tyrone looked at each other and nodded. "We're ready," they said.

Mr. Saber looked at Tim, then at the other boys. "Where's your bottle of water?" Mr. Saber said.

"Um, I don't have one," Tim said. "No one said anything about water." He looked at the other boys. Each of them had a bottle of water in a sling around their shoulders.

"It's always a good idea to bring water on a hike," Brent said. "Dehydration could ruin your day out there."

"It's okay," Paul said. "I've got plenty. Tim can share mine."

"Okay," Mr. Saber said. He looked at his watch. "I'm going to head back to the blanket. Both your caches are about half a mile from this spot, so it should be a fair race."

"Are you going to tell us when to go?" Brent asked.

"Yes," Mr. Saber said. "Get ready."

Tim looked into the woods. The path they were standing on went in pretty deep. But he'd been to this park dozens of times before.

Just a few yards down, the path started to be overgrown with weeds. Beyond that, there was no real path at all. They'd be running through thick forest.

Mr. Saber put up three fingers to count down. "Ready, set . . . ," he said. "Go!"

CHAPTER 5

OFF THE TRAIL

Tim breathed hard as he ran. "We're getting close, I think," he said, looking down at the GPS device. It showed their location and the location of the cache.

"Did you know we're using satellites for this?" Paul said as they ran.

"What?" Tim said. Now that they'd left the main trail, the ground was uneven and soaking wet. Before long, his running shoes proved to be a bad choice.

"Ugh," Tim said. "This is disgusting."

"What?" Paul asked.

"My shoes are all soaked and muddy," Tim explained.

"Why'd you wear running shoes?" Paul asked. "You should have worn some good hiking boots."

"I didn't even know we were going to be doing this," Tim said. He grimaced. "I thought this was going to be a fun day at the beach, remember?"

"Don't worry," Paul said. "Look at it this way. If we get to the cache fast, and make it back first, that'll just mean more time on the beach."

"Yeah, you're right," Tim says. "Okay. Let's try to go as fast as we can."

Tim did his best to step on drier spots, but it was hopeless. His shoes were completely soaked. He knew that because of his wet shoes, he'd have a lot of blisters in the morning.

This better be worth it, he thought grumpily.

"What did you say about satellites?" he asked.

"Oh yeah, satellites," Paul said. "They're owned by the government, I guess. That device you're holding sends signals up there and receives signals. That's how it knows where we are on the planet. Satellites are keeping track of the device."

"Crazy," Tim said. "All for this game?"

"No," Paul said. "They were for some government thing. Spying, maybe."

"I thought satellites were for TV," Tim said.

Paul shrugged. "Anyway, someone thought it would be fun to use them for this, not just for like, government stuff," he said. "Just a few days after they were turned on, this guy put up a website, and bam! Geocaching was born."

"So you learned all this at computer camp?" Tim asked.

"Yup," Paul said.

"Huh," Tim said. He looked down at the device. "Hey, we're here."

The boys stopped and looked around. "So," Tim said, "where is it?"

"Sometimes they're hard to find," Paul said.

"I thought the point of the device was to help us find it," Tim said.

"Yeah," Paul said. "Sort of. The device helps us find the location. But we still have to find the cache."

"I guess we have to look around, then," Tim said.

The boys started wandering around in the small clearing. They lifted up rocks, dug through fallen leaves, and checked under shrubs and mossy logs.

After ten minutes, Tim wanted to give up. He couldn't find anything. His shoes were still soaking, and he was getting dirty.

"This is ridiculous," Tim said. "I can't find anything but leaves and dirt."

"It has to be here," Paul said.

"Unless someone stole it, or something," Tim said.

Paul put his hands on his hips. "Well, I can't find it," he said. "But I do know one thing: we are deep, deep in the woods."

Tim was on his knees, digging through some leaves. He looked up. They were in a tiny clearing, surrounded by trees, with one giant tree right in the middle. The thick growth blocked the sunlight. It was almost like twilight, even though it was not even dinnertime yet.

"Wow, we sure are," Tim said. "I don't even recognize this place."

He stood up and looked around. Then he said, "I hope we can find our way back."

CHAPTER 6

HIGH UP

Even though they were in the shade, it was getting very hot.

Tim took a swig from Paul's bottle of water. "Wow, I am thirsty," he said. "I didn't think I'd get so thirsty in the woods, especially so close to the lake. I'm going to take a break from searching." He sat down on a fallen log.

"Giving up?" Paul said. He was walking in a circle around the edge of the clearing.

"Just taking a break," Tim said. "I'm getting a little sick of this."

He put his head back and took a long chug of water. As he looked up at the sky, he spotted something.

There was a twinkle coming from one of the trees. When he looked closer, he saw that it was perched on a branch. And it wasn't a bird.

"Hey, what's that?" Tim asked.

"What's what?" Tyrone said.

Tim pointed up into the tall tree in the center of the clearing. "Right there," he said. "Something's twinkling on that branch."

Paul went over to Tim and looked up. "I see it," Paul said. "Between those branches. Right?"

Tim nodded. "Do you think someone put the cache all the way up there?" he asked.

"It's possible," Paul said. "I've heard they're sometimes really hard to find. There's one in Antarctica, even."

"The south pole?" Tim said in disbelief.

"Yep," Paul said.

"So how do we get it down?" Tim asked, gazing up at the cache.

Paul looked up at the tree. "We should probably get help, or forget about it," he said. "That thing is way too high up for us to reach."

Paul started walking back in the direction of the beach.

"What?" Tim said. "And let Brent win the prize?"

He got up from the log and walked over to the tree. "No way," Tim said. "We can get it ourselves."

"How?" Paul said.

"We'll climb up and get it," Tim said. "Obviously."

Paul stared up at the cache, twinkling on the branch above them. "Okay," he said finally. "But I'm not going to be the one to climb up there."

"Give me a boost," Tim said. "If I can get up to the lowest branch, I can climb the rest of the way."

Paul seemed unsure, but he shrugged and went over to the tree.

"One, two, three," Tim said. Paul boosted him up with his hands.

With a little work and a stretch, Tim got both hands on the bottom branch. Grunting, he pulled himself up and took a seat.

"Made it," he called down. "Easy."

Tim got to his feet on the branch. He kept one hand on the trunk of the tree and looked up. He could still see the twinkling light above him.

It wasn't too far now, and he could tell it was a small metal box.

"Yup," he called down. "That's definitely the cache. Give me two minutes, and I'll toss it down."

"Okay. Be careful!" Paul said.

Tim wrapped his arms around the trunk and shimmied up a little, just enough to grab the next branch.

Working like that, Tim climbed another ten feet up until he was at the branch with the cache at its end.

"You're really high!" Paul called up. "Be careful!"

"Yeah, yeah," Tim shouted down.

He took a slow step onto the branch. It shook a little, but it was pretty thick.

"Not far now," he whispered to himself. But the branch was shaking a lot. He got down and crawled a little more.

Just then, he heard a crack.

"Whoa," he said quietly.

"You okay?" Paul called up. "I heard a crack."

"Yeah," Tim said. "I have to concentrate."

Tim crawled out a little more and tried to reach for the box. It was still a foot or more out of his grasp.

He took a deep breath and crawled out another couple of inches.

Crack!

"Careful!" Paul called up.

Tim held on tight to the branch. He looked down at Paul.

Paul was way down there, he realized suddenly. If this branch broke, Tim could really get hurt.

The box looked close now. "Maybe I can just tap it," he said to himself. "Then it will fall, and Paul can get it, sign the log, and throw it back up."

It seemed like a good plan.

Tim leaned forward as far as he could, reached out his arm, and . . .

CRACK!

The branch shook violently and bent, then snapped. Tim fell.

CHAPTER 7

MY TURN

Tim threw out his arms and grabbed the next branch. He held on with all his strength, dangling twenty feet up in the tree.

Down below, Paul called, "Are you okay?"

"Yeah, I'm fine," Tim said.

The branch with the cache on it dangled next to him. It had snapped, but was hanging on to the tree by just a splinter.

The cache was only a few feet away from Tim.

"I can reach it!" Tim called down. He took one hand off the branch and reached out toward the cache.

It was too far. There was no way he could reach it.

"Don't move!" Paul called up. "Forget the cache!"

Tim's hand started to slip. Quickly, he put his other hand back on the branch.

"Can you get back to the trunk?" Paul said.

"I think so," Tim said. He turned and put one hand over the other. Soon he could wrap his arms around the trunk. He shimmied down until he was on a nice strong branch, closer to the ground.

Tim sat on the branch, then lowered himself down, dangled for a minute, and dropped to the soft forest ground.

He got up and patted the leaves off his clothes.

"You okay?" Paul said.

"I'm fine," Tim said. The boys looked up at the tree. The cache was still dangling there, out of reach.

"I can't believe someone put it way up there," Tim said.

"It's not worth it," Paul said. "Let's just head back to the beach."

Tim shook his head. "No way," he said. "I want that prize." He walked over to the tree. "Give me another boost," he said.

"No way!" Paul said.

Tim stopped and turned around. Paul was shaking his head. "I'm not letting you go up there again," Paul said. "No way. You could've broken your neck."

"I'm not going back to the beach without the cache," Tim said.

Paul took a deep breath. Then he said, "Fine. I'll go."

Tim raised an eyebrow. "Are you sure?" he asked. "You saw what happened to me."

Paul nodded. "I'm sure," he said. "We're a team. I should be the one to try this time."

He walked over to the tree. "Give me a boost," he said.

CHAPTER 8

Tim helped Paul grab onto the lowest branch. Paul climbed higher. But when he got to a sitting position on a branch just out of reach of the cache, he looked down at Tim.

"I don't think I can do this," Paul whispered.

"Sure you can," Tim said. "You've already made it pretty far. You only have to climb up one more branch."

Paul looked up at the cache. Then he shook his head. "No, I can't do it," he said. "I really can't."

Tim sighed. "It's not a big deal," he said. "Just come on back down."

Paul's face turned red. "I can't," he said again. "I'm really scared of heights."

Tim threw up his hands. "Then why did you climb up there?" he asked.

Paul shrugged. He looked up at the cache, twinkling in the branch above him. "I guess because I knew you really wanted the prize," he said quietly. "And I wanted to make sure our team got it. I thought I could do it. I thought I wouldn't be scared."

"Okay," Tim said. "It's not a big deal. We'll get you out of there. I'll just go get Mr. Saber."

Paul's eyes got wide. "No way," he said. "You can't leave me here."

"I'll be back in, like, twenty minutes," Tim said, trying to keep his voice calm. But inside he was starting to worry. He was worried about Paul. Plus, he wasn't sure what time it was. If they were still out in the woods when it got dark, it could be really hard to find their way back to the beach.

Paul shook his head. "Seriously, Tim," he said. "Please don't leave."

Tim took a deep breath. "Okay," he said. He looked at the tree. There was no way he'd be able to get to the first branch without someone to help him up. And he didn't think Paul would be able to get down alone. He was too scared.

Then Tim slapped his forehead. "Of course!" he said. "Why didn't I think of this before?"

"What?" Paul asked nervously.

Tim reached into his pocket and pulled out his cell phone. "Whew," he said. "I still get service out here." He quickly called Brent's number.

After a couple of rings, Brent picked up. "If you're calling to tell me you're almost back to the beach, you're too late," Brent said. "We already won!"

Tim shook his head. "I'm not," he said. "I'm calling because I need help. Paul and I are at the cache spot we were sent to. Problem is, the cache is in a tree, and Paul's stuck."

He heard Brent take a deep breath.

"Yikes," Brent said. "Dad's swimming. Should I wait for him to get back?"

"I don't think there's time for that," Tim said.

"Okay," Brent said. "Tyrone and I are on our way. Should we just walk straight to the cache, or is there anything in the way, like a river or anything?"

"Nope, nothing like that," Tim said. He glanced up at Paul, and added, "Just get here as fast as you can."

CHAPTER 9

THE PLAN

It took twenty minutes for Tyrone and Brent to find Paul and Tim. When they arrived, they were sweaty and out of breath from running through the woods.

"That was pretty easy," Brent said. "Man, what did people do before GPS existed?"

Tim shrugged. "Do you think we can get Paul down?" he asked quietly, pointing up at their friend in the tree.

Brent and Tyrone stared up at Paul. "Yeah, I think we can," Brent said.

"What are you guys going to do?" Paul asked nervously.

Brent looked at Paul. "Just leave it to us, buddy," he said. Then he turned to Tyrone and Tim. "Here's the plan," he said. "Tim and I will climb up. I'll start down the tree before Paul does. That way, he'll know there's always someone right below him. Just in case. Then he and Tim will climb down at the same time."

Tim looked at Paul. "Did you hear that?" he asked. "Do you think it'll work?"

Paul nodded slowly. "I think so," he said.

Tyrone boosted Brent and Tim into the tree. Tim climbed all the way up to Paul. Brent stayed a branch below them.

Slowly, Paul crept down. Sometimes he'd look down at the ground and shiver or close his eyes. Then Tyrone, Brent, or Tim would tell him he could do it.

It took about ten minutes before all four boys were standing in a circle on the ground.

"You made it!" Tyrone said, giving his brother a high five.

"I guess so," Paul said. "I wouldn't have if it hadn't been for you guys," he added.

"But you did," Tim said. "And now I think we should get back to the beach. We all earned some relaxation time!"

CHAPTER 10

Back at the beach, the boys told Mr. Saber what had happened. Brent's dad shook his head. "You guys did the right thing, getting out of there without trying to get the cache one more time," he said. "Sometimes caches are hard to reach. On the website, that cache wasn't listed as difficult, though. It should have been."

Brent nodded. "You both could've gotten hurt," he said.

Tim nodded. "But we didn't," he said. "And I have to admit, this proved that geocaching is pretty exciting. We should try it again."

"Only not in a place with so many trees," Paul added. Everyone laughed.

"So how did you guys do?" Tim asked Brent and Tyrone.

"We got to our cache and signed the book," Brent said. "Therefore, we won the prize."

He and Tyrone high-fived. Then Brent added, "Plus, check this out."

Brent dug into his pocket and pulled out what looked like a big fishing lure.

Tim took it and looked it over. "What is it?" he asked.

"It's a travel bug," Brent said. "Some caches have them inside. You can go to the website and register that you found it, and then you put it inside a cache you find in the future. The person who first planted the bug gets to watch it move all over the country. We'll go look this one up when we get home, and we might find it started clear across the country."

"Or the world," Tim said. "There's a cache in Antarctica, you know."

Brent and his dad laughed. "Sounds like you're beginning to get into this geocaching stuff, huh?" Brent said.

Tim shrugged, but he smiled too. "I guess so," he said. "It's pretty cool. The satellites, the hunt, traveling all over the world. I didn't realize how much there was to it, I guess."

Tim could smell the dinner barbecue was already being fired up. Soon the sun would set, and the fireworks would begin.

"Well," Tim said, standing next to Paul, "I guess we didn't win the prize."

Paul shrugged. "No big deal. Tyrone was on the winning team, so I'm sure he'll let me use it, whatever it is."

Mr. Saber looked at Brent. Brent nodded. Then Mr. Saber pulled out the small, wrapped box again. "Well, Tim," he said, "Tyrone and Brent and I talked it over. We decided you should get the prize after all."

"What?" Tim said. "But we didn't even sign our log. I don't deserve the prize."

Mr. Saber handed him the box. "Trust me," he said. "It makes sense for you to have it."

"Um, okay," Tim said. He took the box. "Thanks."

Tim pulled the brown paper off the box. Inside was a brand-new GPS device. "Wow," he said. "This is amazing. Thanks, Mr. Saber. But I can't accept it. I didn't win."

Brent shrugged. "We already have GPS devices," he said. "Now you can join us next weekend for another hunt."

Tim smiled. "Sounds good to me," he said. "I actually can't wait!"

"School's starting tomorrow," Brent said. "It'll be awesome to have this to look forward to on the weekends."

"Yeah it will," Paul said. "And we can even do it in the winter."

"I think I need to get some better shoes," Tim said, laughing.

ABOUT THE AUTHOR

Eric Stevens lives in St. Paul, Minnesota with his wife, dog, and son. He is studying to become a teacher. Some of his favorite things include pizza and video games. Some of his least favorite things include olives and shoveling snow.

ABOUT THE ILLUSTRATOR

When Sean Tiffany was growing up, he lived on a small island off the coast of Maine. Every day until he graduated from high school, he had to take a boat to get to school! Sean has a pet cactus named Jim.

GLOSSARY

ANNUAL (AN-yoo-uhl)—something that happens every year

CACHE (KASH)—a hiding place or something hidden

CELEBRATION (sel-uh-BRAY-shuhn)—a happy gathering

COORDINATES (koh-OR-duh-nits)—a set of numbers used to show the position of a point on a line, graph, or map

DEVICE (di-VISSE)—a piece of equipment that does a particular job

GEOCACHING (JEE-oh-kash-ing)—using GPS coordinates to locate a hidden cache

GOVERNMENT (GUHV-urn-muhnt)—the people who rule or govern a country

GPS (JEE PEE ESS)—short for Global Positioning System, a system that uses satellites to help users determine their location

LOCATION (loh-KAY-shuhn)—the place where something is

LOG (LOG)—a written record of something

SATELLITES (SAT-uh-lites)—spacecrafts that are sent into orbit around the earth and transmit signals

DISCUSSION QUESTIONS

1. Tim wanted to swim, but Brent wanted to go geocaching. Talk about a time that you and your friend wanted to do different things. What happened? What else could Tim and Brent have done to make sure they had a fun day?

2. Have you gone geocaching? If not, would you like to? Talk about it.

3. When Paul was scared in the tree, what else could Tim have done to help him?

WRITING PROMPTS

1. Tim and his friends celebrate the end of summer with a barbecue at the beach. How do you feel at the end of summer? Write about what you do before the school year begins.

2. Paul is afraid of heights. Write about something you're afraid of. How do you get over your fear?

3. Pretend you're a newspaper reporter. Write an article about the events that happen in this book. Don't forget to include a headline!

MORE ABOUT

According to Geocaching.com, there are more than 4 million geocachers worldwide, searching for more than 1.2 million caches. The caches are placed all over the world.

Geocaching works using GPS. GPS stands for Global Positioning System. To function, it uses satellites. The satellites pick up information from GPS devices and relay information back to the devices. The satellites figure out where the device is on the planet. Then, they're able to direct geocachers to the caches.

Geocaching first started getting popular in 2000. A man named Dave Ulmer wanted to test how well GPS devices worked, so he hid a black bucket in the woods near Beavercreek, Oregon. Then he gave some other GPS users the bucket's coordinates. That was the first cache.

GEOCACHING

The best thing for a new geocacher to do is just start looking for caches! Buy or borrow a GPS device, and use the Internet to find caches near you. (Of course, make sure an adult is aware of what you're doing.)

Start out with an easy cache, and work your way up to harder ones. Before you know it, you'll be a geocaching pro!